TRACIE'S INHERITANCE

A NOVEL

BY

G. LAWRENCE

2004 by Glenn L. Garrett, Publisher

Library of Congress Cataloging-in-Publication Data

Glenn L. Garrett

Tracie's Inheritance : a novel by G. Lawrence

Second Edition - 2004

Published by Glenn L. Garrett
215-549-7724
email - glenn.garrett@verizon.net

ISBN: 1-59196-383-4

Printed in the United States of America

TABLE OF CONTENTS

CHAPTER 1

HOW IT ALL BEGAN

It was a cold winter's night, but the Freeman family was cozy and warm in their house. Each one involved in his own little project, including little Courtney, who was curled up like a little, furry, ball in front of the television. Fast asleep! Her sister, Brittany, sat on the sofa watching the television with her little toes tucked up under. Her brother, Marcus? Well, he was doing what he usually did, which was to play his video games on the computer in the sitting room.

When the doorbell rang, it startled everyone.

"Oh my goodness!", said Brittany, "That thing scared me to death. I'll get it." she said.

But as she started for the door, her father stopped her. His name was Christopher but everyone called him Chris for short. He had decided that it was best to answer the door himself.

"No, no baby, that's all right, I'll get it. It's late and you never know who's at that door this time of night. Hey, what's that you're watching anyway?" he asked, as he passed the television. "That looks like something you shouldn't even be watching!"

"Aw Daddy this is 90201. This is a great show. It's about...Oh never mind." She stopped talking and turned back to watching the program because she saw that her father was no longer paying her any attention as he continued toward the door.

Chris looked through the little peephole in the door, he squinted to see who it was. He always did this before opening it, because it was safe and he told his children to always *ask* who was there before opening the door.

"Who is it?" Chris called.

"Can't you see, man? I know you're lookin' right at my face through that little hole," he heard the voice say from the other side of the door. He thought he recognized the voice, so he opened the door. He was so surprised. It was Scoota. He hadn't seen Scoota in a very long time and he was very happy to see him. A broad grin spread across his face as he greeted him.

"Scoota? Scoota! My man! Man, I didn't know who you were, at first. I can't *see* nothin' these days. What's happenin' man? Come on in. Come on in here, boy, it's cold out there." He shook Scoota's hand and hugged him as they stood just inside the doorway.

"You right! You can't see because you're getting old. That's why," Scoota said. It was easy to tell by the look on their faces that they were very happy to see one another.

Chris laughed and agreed with Scoota that he was getting older and that was indeed the reason he hadn't been seeing very well. "Man. How you been? What you doin' way down here in Atlanta, Georgia, anyway? You're a mighty long way from Philly."

"Shoot, I'm all over the place these days," Scoota replied, "Just thought I'd drop in and see y'all while I was here, that's all. Now where's Tracie and the kids? That's who I *really* came to see. Not you!"

Chris knew that Scoota was only kidding, but he pretended as though he didn't know.

"Aw, you know you missed me, don't even act like that. Hey! Hold on I'll call her for you. Tracie!" Chris called out. "Tracie! Get off that phone and come here and see who it is. That woman is forever on the phone," he remarked.

He took Scoota's heavy coat, scarf and hat and hung them in the closet which was right next to the door.

"Come on man, don't just stand there, it's cold here, too, I know you gotta' be cold in that short sleeve shirt."

As he and Scoota walked toward the living room, they were met by Tracie. She had cut her telephone conversation short because she was anxious to see who it was also.

3

When she saw that it was Scoota, she stopped right in her tracks. "Lawd, will you look at this?" she said in a surprised voice. "Well if it ain't Scoota. Scoota look at you! You ain't changed a bit in all these years. You still look the same. Come here and give me some hug." She, too, was very happy to see him. She hugged him and jumped up and down like a little girl who was just given something she always wished for.

"What you doing here in Georgia? Why didn't you call and tell us you were coming? I coulda'..."

"Hey. Hold up. Gimme' a chance to say somethin', here." Scoota chimed in, "Man. Let me look at you. Shoot, girl, you the one who ain't changed. You still look as young and pretty as you did back in the day. It's good to see you. It's good to see you both but, now, where them two little guys at?" He began to look around on the floor and around the room as if he was looking for something he lost.

"Oh Scoota come on. Now, you *know* we got *three* children, not two," she playfully tugged at Scoota's arm as if she were angry with him, although she really wasn't.

"Brittany! Marcus! Come here and see who it is."

They both were too involved in what they were doing to even have heard all the clambering at the door. Both children came.

"Uncle Scoota!" said Brittany, as a smile brightened her face. She immediately jumped into his arms and hugged him tight around his neck.

"Whoa. Girl, you are too big and heavy to be jumpin' up on me like that." Scoota said, but he continued to hold her and she squeezed him even tighter him around his neck.

"What's up, Uncle Scoota?" asked Marcus, who was a little less excited. Then again, Marcus didn't get excited over anything unless it was a video game or football.

"Hey Mark. Dag! Look at you! Man, you sure got big."

Marcus looked at Chris as though he had seen a ghost.

"Dag man. What you feedin' them kids?" Everybody laughed. It was a very happy moment.

They pulled "Uncle" Scoota into the living room and sat him down on the sofa. Chris went to fix up a pot of herb tea, which he knew Scoota liked. Tracie sat down in the chair that faced the sofa and tried to talk to Scoota while Brittany sat on his lap. They took turns talking back and forth to Scoota. Marcus, though, stood directly in front of him until he finally got a chance to say what he wanted to say. He just stood there...smiling. Then he said it.

"You know what I'm gonna ask you don't you?" Marcus asked as the smile grew wider on his face.

"Aw no. Noooo. I know just what you gone say. No. I ain't got time." Scoota knew what Marcus was hinting about. He knew Marcus was hinting about his favorite sub-ject, his very own mother and father. He knew that Scoota knew what he was talking about, too, because every time they saw Uncle Scoota they asked him to do it.

"Aw please?" Marcus begged, "Come on Uncle Scoota. Please? Just a little bit?"

"At this point, Brittany caught on and she, too, began to plead along with Marcus. Together, they began to put the pressure on Uncle Scoota to tell the story.

Okay! That's enough. Can't you guys see that Uncle Scoota is tired? Maybe he doesn't feel like telling that story right now." Chris walked in with the tea and placed it on the coffee table in front of Scoota as he spoke to the children. He, too, knew what they were up to."

"Your daddy's right," added Tracie, "give Uncle Scoota a break. He just got in the door. Why don't you guys get ready for bed anyway? It's almost eight thirty. Look, your little sister is already sound asleep on the floor. Maybe Uncle Scoota will tell you the story tomorrow." She turned her attention to Scoota, "You are going to stay here tonight? Aren't you?"

"Oh! Uh, no.see uh, I got to get back to my friend's house. See, she don't live too far from y'all and... ."

The children ignored his feeble excuse and they attacked him even harder, begging him to tell them the story that they loved so well.

The story they so wanted to hear was one that Uncle Scoota knew well because he was a big part of it. To them it was one of the greatest stories they ever heard because it was the story of how their mother and father first fell in love and got married. Besides, Uncle Scoota had a way of telling it that really made it come to life.

"Please. Please Daddy. Let him tell us just a little bit of it? Ooooo, oooo Uncle Scoota just tell us the part where you found mommy in your house, and she scared you. Please? Just that part and we'll go to bed, we promise!" Marcus begged.

"Chris. Gimme' a little help here. These kids just don't give up. Do they?"

"Come on Marcus. Give Uncle Scoota a break, he's tired. Maybe tomorrow he can come back and tell it."

Tracie picked up little Courtney and was upstairs putting her to bed. She was the one who really controlled the kids, and the kids knew this. They also knew if they kept it up long enough that their father would give in and let them have their way. They pleaded so much that *Scoota* finally gave in. Daddy never said a word. It was plain to see that he liked the story as well.

"Okay. Okay. But only the real short version, and then I'm going to stop, because I have got to go. Okay?"

They were very excited. Marcus plopped down right in front of Scoota, and Brittany climbed down off his lap and sat down next to him. They made themselves comfortable and ready to listen. Then, out of nowhere, Brittany asked, "Oooo, tell us the part where..." Scoota held up his hand to Brittany just as she started to speak.

"Hold on there. Now are you going to let me tell this story or what? Huh? Okay! No more interruptions...okay? Okay. Now, it's like this!" He began the story...

"Now lets see, it was back in about 1967," he began, "your father was working for his father in their funeral home, Freeman's Funeral Parlor. Used to be up on Seventeenth Street in Philly.

"Now, one day his pop sent him out to the rich folks' neighborhood to pick up some papers or somethin'. He had just gotten a brand, spankin' new car. And he was very proud of it. It was made in his favorite colors, red and white. Well, he had just finished washing it all up and stuff, and he just couldn't wait to take it out on the street and drive it. So, anyway, he hopped in it I guess he just got to thinking that he was so pretty in it that he musta' forgot where he was goin'. Way up in Bala Cynwyd somewhere. Well, wouldn't you know it? He got lost. That's right, lost! He didn't know where he was or where he was goin'. Anyway, he ended up driving down this real nice country road. Trees on every side and lots of green lawns..."

Brittany was listening very intently. She loved this story because she heard it so many times that she knew it by heart. She began to picture, in her mind, everything that Uncle Scoota was telling them. She could easily imagine the car and her father in it and the nice country road winding through the countryside. She could envision everything, and not only that, she knew every word of the story as though she had been there herself and had heard every word. She had a habit of daydreaming while she listened to stories. This way, she could not only *hear* the story as it was being told, but she could *watch* it unfold in her mind. God had blessed her with a great imagination so she could see the story just as though she were sitting in a movie theater watching it.

That was the best part about stories for her. She could actually see them take place right there in her head. She didn't even have to be there. She could just imagine it, and it was just as real to her.

"Well", Scoota continued, "on the very same day that Chris got lost, guess what? It also happened to be your mother's seventeenth birthday. Her mother and father let her have a party, so she had some of her girlfriends over, and they were having a good time, dancing and singing and eating cake and ice cream and drinking juice and stuff. Then it started to get late and everybody had to get ready and go home. So, anyway, when the party was over, your mother's father, Mr. Phillips. At least that's what we all called him. He was your grandfather. Well, he called her to his side and told her that he had some very good news to tell her and that he had some very bad news to tell her."

Brittany began to drift. She was rapidly being sucked into the magic land of imagination, that world where she could be anything she wanted to be. She could see her mother sitting in the very same place she sat when her father gave her the good news and the bad news. She had been to Philly and seen the house before so she knew what it looked like. She could even hear the words her grandfather was telling her mother. All this was beginning to take place in her mind. It was as if Uncle Scoota's voice had trailed off and now she was actually hearing the voice of her grandfather. It was magical, and it was beginning to be real for little Brittany. Her imagination had taken over....

CHAPTER 2

Good News, Bad News

U mmm boy this is some really good punch," Mr. Phillips said to little Tracie. I hope you had a good time at your party. Uh, honey, you know I love you very much. Don't you? Well, come here and sit down beside Daddy and let me talk to you for a minute. I have something very important I want to tell you."

Tracie was given a cute little puppy as one of her birthday presents. She named him Kibble. He had soft, curly, black fur and was really cuddly. She carried him everywhere she went. She really loved Kibble from the very first moment she saw him. She scooped up little Kibble and stroked his shiny, black coat as she skipped over to where her father was sitting. Little Tracie truly enjoyed sitting with her father. They talked often, but this time she had a feeling it was going to be a different kind of talk. So she asked him, "Is something wrong daddy?"

"No. There's nothing *wrong*, honey, but let's just say I got some good news and I got some bad news to tell you. Let me see. How should I begin this? Okay. As you know, your grandmother is very ill, and, at this point, she is not doing so well in the hospital. The doctors tell us that she is very sick. That's the reason we're going to Baltimore tomorrow. To see her. Well, she is the one that we can thank for us living as well as we do today. You *do* know we live pretty well don't you? We have this nice big house, and you have all the clothes you want, and we give you just about everything you want. Right?

"We don't have a problem with money! No sir. We live better than most. And that's because of your grandmother. You see, she had a lot of land left to her by her father, and she sold the land and made a lot of money off of it. After your mother and I got married, she gave us a great deal of money. And I used that money to start my own real-estate business. Thank the Good Lord, I have been very fortunate with my investments. Well, she also set aside a tidy little sum of money for you. About two-hundred thousand dollars at that time. Now with interest, and what not, that sum has grown to be considerably more. Upon you reaching your eighteenth birthday, next year, you will be eligible to receive this money, provided you meet two conditions. One condition is that you must be eighteen years old. And the other condition is that you must be enrolled in college."

"Daddy that's a lot of money," she said excitedly "I'll never be able to spend all that. But that's such good news I don't see how anything else you say could be bad. What's the bad news? That's what I want to hear." She seemed even more eager to hear the bad news.

"Well, first of all, I didn't say it was going to be easy to get this money. As a matter of fact, I think you may have a lot of problems with it. You remember Evellia, Don't you?"

"Oh yes of course," said Tracie. "She's my beautiful step-sister. I remember her. She loves me, and she always tells me how pretty I am."

"Oh boy. I don't know about all of that, but anyway, as it turns out, Evellia has long been suspected of having something to do with my first wife's death. You see, when I was married the first time, Evellia was my only child. And she was very moody and bossy. As she grew up, she got to messin' around with that black magic and voodoo stuff. I don't know if you know about that but, in some countries, they don't recognize the same God as we do. They have their own religion and it's called voodoo or Juju or black magic. We don't like it. So, anyway, she forgot all about going to church and God and Jesus and all the good things we taught her. She never liked nobody tellin' her what to do anyway. One day when I came home, I found Evellia standing over my wife chanting some weird kind of words. My wife died shortly after that. The doctors couldn't figure out what she died from. It was very mysterious but your grandmother blamed her for my wife's death, consequently, she only left her one penny in her will. That's all! Just one little penny. Well, Evellia now knows about this, and she has vowed to get what she thinks is her share of the money. Plus, she has vowed to get you, because she has always felt that since I remarried, and had you, that you were my favorite and that's why you got the bigger part of the estate. She is an evil child. She does not like you. And she will do everything in her power to get the money your grandmother left to you so that she can have it all to herself. So you must beware of her. She is not to be trusted at all. And that's the long and short of it."

He finished telling Tracie the good news and the bad news.
Poor little Tracie was stunned. She couldn't even find words
to speak, this was so unbelievable.

"Oh my God. You can't mean that Evellia would try
to...I mean, she couldn't...she wouldn't try to hurt me..."
Tracie was so very upset over the thought of someone trying
to harm her that she just couldn't even say it. The thought of
it being her sister made matters worse. *How could she*, she
thought, her very own sister. Even though they had different mothers, she always thought of Evellia as her big sister.
She could not stop the tears from flowing down her face.
Tracie got up as though she were in a trance. She picked up
her little puppy and walked out onto the porch. There she
sat, thinking and crying. She was very sad. And little
Kibble was sad with her.

As she sat crying, she never noticed the shiny, red,
and white Buick Electra 225 drive quietly up to the porch.
The man who was driving was Chris. He got out and stood
by the door of the car. He looked around at the spacious
house and the winding road he had just come up. But when
he saw Tracie, his heart skipped a beat. She was beautiful.
He thought she looked like and angel. And he couldn't take
his eyes off of her.

"Uh, excuse me ma'am." he stuttered, "but could
you?..." Then he stopped. He stopped because he noticed
the tears in her eyes and the sadness in her face. But beside
that, he saw something much deeper in her eyes. Something
heavenly. He saw her beauty, and he saw how pretty she
was. He was truly smitten. It was as if he had forgotten how
to talk.

She heard his voice and looked up. At first, she was shocked at his being there, then, realizing that she was crying like a baby, she became embarrassed.

"Who are you?" she asked in a surprised tone. "No. I don't know, I just don't know... . Please go away."

Upon saying this, she turned and ran back into the house leaving a very distraught Chris standing there looking at her disappear into the house. He had forgotten all about the fact that he was lost. He even forgot what he was supposed to be doing. He could only think of this beautiful face he'd just seen. It was as if he were hypnotized and in a trance. He had no idea how long he had been standing there before he finally made his way to the car and drove back down the winding path that lead to the main road. Looking back all the while, hoping to catch just one more glimpse of the angel.

CHAPTER 3
TRADEGY STRIKES

Morning came and the Phillips were packed and ready to take their trip to Baltimore. Of course Tracie and little Kibble were the last ones out of the house, and Tracie was the only one who had three pieces of luggage. More than everybody else, Mrs. Phillips was flabbergasted.

"My goodness Tracie, you didn't have to try to bring everything you owned," Mrs. Phillips joked. "Help her with that Henry. You know she can't lift that onto the top of that car." He huffed and sighed as though he were tired but at the same time he helped Tracie load her bags onto the top of the station wagon. Once they were packed up, they all got into the car and started out on their journey to Baltimore."

At this point, Brittany snapped out of her daydream. She was suddenly brought back to reality.

"Oh no! Uncle Scoota. I don't like this part. It always makes me cry." She said sadly. "I have to go to the bathroom. Don't tell any more 'til I get back." And she darted upstairs.

When she got up to go to the bathroom, Scoota decided to take a break as well. He sat back in his chair, crossed his legs and sipped on his tea. Tracie had returned from putting Courtney to bed and was just about to tell Marcus to get ready to go up. Well, uncle Scoota saved the day for them. He quickly suggested that Marcus go put on his pajamas and tell Brittany to do the same. They all looked at him with relief because they knew that he had saved them from having to go to bed.

They knew that when they all came back, it would be alright, they would already be prepared for bed and they could just jump right in after the story. Marcus happily flew up the stairs and told Brittany what to do. All this talking woke Courtney up. So now when they came down the steps, there were three.

"Hey. Look who's up." shouted Uncle Scoota. "Come on over here and give Uncle Scoota a kiss and a hug."

Courtney was only three years old and she didn't remember Uncle Scoota as well as Marcus and Brittany. She didn't know that uncle Scoota was the best story teller ever. Marcus was eight and Brittany was six so they had known him a little longer. Besides, Courtney was shy around "strangers". So she didn't come to Uncle Scoota. Instead she sidled up to daddy. She had her thumb in her mouth as she leaned on her father's knee, never taking her eyes off of Uncle Scoota.

"Okay. Be like that then." Scoota remarked to Courtney, "I'll just tell them the rest of the story and you won't hear it."

He was joking with her to try to make friends with her. He knew she would hear him anyway, as he told the story.

"Ok Uncle Scoota, we ready." Marcus said.

They had rearranged themselves around their daddy's legs as they sat on the floor. Courtney too had joined them. They were ready for Uncle Scoota to continue the story.

"Ok. This is it. The next time I stop I'm going out the door. Y'all got that?" He looked at each one of them as he spoke and shook his finger at them in turn. He could sense that little Courtney was warming up to him already because she smiled at him.

"Now where was I? Oh, Tracie and her family were gettin' ready to go to Baltimore, but somebody had too many bags." He glanced at Tracie, who also was listening to the story.

Brittany slipped very easily back into her imaginary world. The world where she was now watching his words turn into pictures. She envisioned the brown station wagon moving along the road. She could plainly hear the happy voices of the family talking as they headed down the highway towards their destination. She didn't like what was to take place next because she had seen it too many times before in her previous imaginings...

"The road was dark and lonely." Scoota continued, "The snow had fallen silently to the ground covering the trees and the grass and everything it lay on. The loud sound of a siren screamed out in the darkness. The only light came from the moon and the headlights of a police car that was parked in the middle of the road." There was a police officer at the scene. There had been an accident. The Phillips' station wagon was overturned and on fire in a gully. The police officer stood on the bank of the gully looking down at the burning metal and rubber. *There's just no hope, he thought.*

And he sadly turned to leave. Just as he turned to go to his vehicle to put in the report, he heard a groan not far from where he was standing. He strained to see in the dim light. Curious, he began to walk in the direction of the noise. As he followed the sounds, he came upon the body of young Tracie. She was hurt badly, but she was alive. Quickly, he administered first aid to her and did everything he could to make her comfortable. When he was sure she was all right he went to his car and called for an ambulance. The ambulance arrived in just minutes. And Tracie was rushed to the hospital where she was given immediate medical care.

She remained in the hospital for three weeks. On the whole, she was all right considering that she suffered a concussion and contusions to her head, a broken leg and some minor cuts and burns. She was recuperating very well when one day her doctor visited her in her room. The doctor's name was Dr. Hoskins."

"Well, Tracie, I see you are awake. How do you feel?" the doctor asked.

"Good morning doctor. I feel pretty good. I guess. I'll just be glad when you can take this cast and these bandages off so I can get out of here." Tracie responded.

"Uh, Tracie, we are working on that now but, uh, as it was most unfortunate that your parents didn't survive, one good thing *has* come out of it. That is, uh, that you won't be left entirely alone.

"You'll be glad to know that we've contacted your sister. And she is eager to help. Isn't that wonderful? It appears that she has graciously assumed legal guardianship over you and she will be taking care of you until you fully recover. She doesn't have a car but she has asked if I would take you home when the time comes. And of course I agreed. Isn't that good of her?"

Young Tracie didn't know what to say. She was shocked at this news. The words of her father rang loudly in her head. "SHE IS EVIL AND NOT TO BE TRUSTED AT ALL".
Fear rushed through her body. She felt a cold sensation upon her skin. Her very blood seemed to run cold through her veins.

"Wait a minute doctor. I don't have a...you mean my stepsister? You mean Evellia? My stepsister, Evellia, is living in my house? Oh my God! This can't be."

"Now don't get upset Tracie. It's going to be all right. Sister; Stepsister, it's all the same. You are just lucky that she will be there for you. Well, I have to check on another patient now but you get some rest and we'll talk more a little later. Ok?"

As the doctor left, a nurse entered and began to do a routine check on Tracie. Tracie lay quietly in a state of disbelief.

Two days passed. Tracie, as yet, was not over the shock of what she had been told. She was trying hard to figure things out when the doctor entered the room. He studied her for a moment and then said to her.

"Uh, Tracie. I think you're ready to leave the hospital now. So tomorrow, I'll be driving you home where your sister is prepared to take care of you. I told her of your concern and she has assured me that you will receive nothing but the best of care. I trust her, Tracie! I really do! And I would hope you will too. It will make things much easier. Now I suggest that you begin packing your things and sometime tomorrow, I will be in to get you. Okay?"

The doctor left before Tracie could utter a word. She was in such an unbelievable state of belief that she just couldn't believe it. She looked at the doctor with her finger pointing to him as he exited the door. Her mouth was open but she was unable to speak.

Night came. She was packed but not at all ready. As she tried to go to sleep she found it very difficult. She kept having little short nightmares that would force her to open her eyes. She finally got to sleep but morning came so fast that she didn't even realize that she slept. The doctor was in the room when she awoke. It all seemed to happen so fast. The next thing she knew she was being pushed in a wheelchair headed toward the doors that lead to the outside and to her home...where she was very reluctant to go.

Tracie and the doctor were driving along in the car. It was almost nightfall and they were drawing closer to the home she once loved. Now, the road seemed eerie. The moon was shining on the white snow reflecting the shadows of the trees onto the road and the ground around it.

It all looked so different. It felt weird. The closer she got to home, the more she noticed that the shadows seemed to take on different shapes. They were almost frightening . They seemed to change shapes right in front of her. She felt very uncomfortable and afraid. As they neared the house, she noticed that it , too, appeared to have changed. It had never looked so dreary and cold before. The wind was blowing unusually hard and it was dark except for the moonlight. The car drove around the culdesac and stopped at the door. The doctor got out of the car and helped Tracie with her baggage. They both stood in front of the door. As the doctor prepared to knock, the door swung open as if by itself, and Evellia appeared. They looked up at her. She was taller than Tracie remembered and her hair was streaked with gray. She was dressed in a slinky, blue, satin, dress and was holding a candle in one hand. The other was poised on the edge of the door. She was looking down at both of them. Her eyes were smeared with black mascara.

"Oooooo! It's little Tracie," she said in a singsong voice. Then she looked at the doctor very sternly as she put the candle down and grabbed Tracie by the shoulder.

"I'll take it from here, doc." she barked at the doctor. And in one quick move, she snatched Tracie inside and slammed the door in the doctor's face. The doctor was stunned. He stood there for a moment trying to figure out what happened.

Then he felt a chill run down his spine. He felt as though eyes were on him. Like something was watching him. He quickly turned and looked around. When he didn't see anything, he dashed for his car and drove hastily away.

Inside the house, Tracie was hearing the weirdest music she had ever heard. At least not in this house had she experienced such harsh notes as those she was hearing now. She was confused. The house didn't look anything like it did when she and her parents left it just four weeks ago.

There were candles everywhere, and they were lit. The furniture was covered with black sheets. And there were mirrors on every wall. Before she could shape her mouth to say anything, Evellia directed her toward the winding staircase. Pushing her along as they reached the top of the stairs. Tracie was further surprised by yet another unfamiliar sight. In what once was her parents bedroom, were still more burning candles. They were all around the room. Even on the bed!

And what was stranger yet, was the old, gray haired, woman sitting crossed legged on the floor. She was wearing a turban on her head and she appeared to be sleep. Sitting up!

"Who is that, Evellia? I don't know her. What is she doing in my mommy's room and why?

EVELLIA

MAUREEN

"Shut up! This is no longer your "mommy's" room?"
Evellia screamed at her. "This is my friend and advisor
Maureen. And you will stay out of here. Do you hear me.
You wretched little snake." Her voice grew more intolerant
and angry as she spoke.

"Maureen tells me of my fortunes and future good
fortunes and all I need to know to preserve my beauty. Now
you get you into your dirty little room and stay there until I
call for you."

She shoved Tracie into the room which she once
adored and closed the door. Tracie heard the key being
inserted from the outside. She knew she was being locked
in. She was shaken by Evellia's unexpected transformation.
Scared and shaken, she sought refuge in a corner. She felt
very alone and frightened as she cowered and looked up at
the window. The moonlight was shining in the window but
it was dark everywhere else. Everywhere except under the
bed. She looked closer. She saw a pair of eyes, green eyes
looking at her. She knew right away what it was. It was
Kibble, her little puppy. He had been hiding under the bed
all the while. He slowly creeped out from under the bed and
came to Tracie. She could see he was very scared, even to
come to her. She crawled over to meet him and picked him
up in her arms. He was shaking violently. She drew him
close to her body and began stroking him, crying all the
while. They comforted each other.

After about an hour in that cold, dark room. She decided to say a prayer. She had been taught that when things don't seem to be going well, the thing to do is to pray. So that's what she did. She got on her knees and lay her hands on the edge of the bed and she prayed. She prayed to God. She prayed for about fifteen minutes. It took her a long time to figure out what to say at first, but she managed to get some words together in her heart, then she said them out of her mouth. Once she finished, it seemed that she began to gather strength. She was even less afraid after that. It was as if she didn't care any more about that house or Evellia or anything else, outside of Kibble. She began to feel that her life was being threatened and she was not about to let anything bad happen to her. She just wasn't ready for that. She decided that since she feared her life was in danger, she was going to make a run for it. She made a plan and got right on it. Her means of escape would be to climb out of the window and down a makeshift 'rope', and run as fast as she could to safety. It was a good plan.

Taking the sheets and covers off the bed, she tied them into knots to make sort of a "rope" out of them. She then tied one end of the 'homemade rope' to the leg of her bed. The other end, she threw out of the window. It was only on the second floor, so she had more than enough to reach the ground below. It was a good plan and it was working. She gathered a few clothes from her closet and wrapped them in a jacket. She tied a knot in the jacket with the sleeves and pushed the tip of an umbrella up through it, so she could carry it easier.

She then picked up little Kibble and began her climb to freedom and safety. Once she hit the snow covered ground, she took off running. Kibble in her arms. Umbrella in hand. She ran as fast as her little legs could carry her. Crying the whole time. Crying. Running. Crying. Running. Slipping. Never looking back.

All the while, Evellia had been thinking of how she was going to dispose of Tracie and get her money. She was standing and gazing into one of the many mirrors she had around the house. There was a sinister, evil look on her face as she reached a conclusion. She always looked in the mirror and adored herself before and after she did anything to please herself. And that's what she did best. Please herself.

She then went to Maureen and made her give her advise. She admired herself in the mirror for about a half hour before going to Maureen. Up the steps she went. Evellia was so vane that she couldn't help but look at herself as she ascended the steps because the steps and the walls going up the steps were mirrored. Pleased with herself and her plan, she smiled.

Maureen remained in the same position she was in when Tracie saw her. Sitting cross-legged on the floor surrounded by candlelight. Her eyes were closed and her hands were clasped between her legs. She sat very still. Evellia crept close to the door and peered in.

"Maureen!" Evellia called in a cross voice. "Now that you've rested, I'd like to know what is in store for me. I want to know if I am still the most beautiful creature upon all the earth? And when will I get my money?" She was glaring down on Maureen who had opened her eyes. Maureen responded the same way she always does. With a chant.

AT YOUR REQUEST, I'LL DO MY BEST
TO SET YOUR HOPES AND FEARS TO REST
THE CARDS WILL TELL IF ALL IS WELL.
AS I RELEASE THE MYSTERIES
OF HEAVEN AND HELL

After she chanted the verse, she fell into a trance-like state. Then, a deck of Tarot cards that had been stacked in front of her mysteriously began to shuffle and deal itself. Once the cards arranged themselves on the floor, a deep tone sounded from out of the air itself.

"Come on Maureen." Evellia prodded, "Come on. Tell me! What do they say? Am I still the best looking woman ever? Am I? What?" She was very demanding as she shook Maureen by her shoulders.

Maureen, unphased by the shaking, looked at the cards that were spread out before her. She then looked up at Evellia. Only the whites of her eyes could be seen and she spoke as though she were in a trance.

ONCE YOU WERE FAIREST YET NEVER FAIR
YOUR DESTINY IS HOLDING BY A STRAND OF HAIR
A LARGE SUM OF MONEY THRU HER BLOOD WILL COME
BUT SHANT BE GIVEN BUT UNTO ONE

Upon hearing these last words, Evellia jumped for joy. The evil joy of thinking that she had been given good news.

"That's it!" she declared "That's alls I needed to hear. Thank you, love! I'm outta here." She headed down the steps happy as a lark. Just about singing the last words she heard from Maureen.

"SHANT BE GIVEN BUT UNTO ONE," she repeated aloud. "Darn right! Only one, and that one will be me. Yes suh, alls I got to do is get rid of that little wretch." Evellia was so overcome with this evil joy that she decided to follow through with her plan immediately. She looked up at the ceiling that is the floor of the room where she thought Tracie to be. She fixed herself a drink made up of a potion she mixed up earlier, turned up the volume of her weird music. Then, she went to the kitchen and got a big knife.

"This is just as good a time as any." she said to herself. And she crept stealthily up the steps to Tracie's room. Sneaking up to the keyhole, she tried to peek in first to see what she could see. But it was too dark. So she quietly inserted the key and turned it trying not to make any noise. She pushed the door open and stepped in.

Once inside, she looked around the room. The first thing she saw was the sheets draped over the windowsill and dangling out. She became enraged. She began to breathe very deeply and loudly. She hadn't notice that she was cutting herself with the knife. When she suddenly felt pain in her leg she looked down and saw blood. The sight of the blood caused her to go further into a frenzy. She dashed to the window and looked down at the clump of material lying in the snow. She saw the little footprints leading away from the house. She was livid. Really mad. She stood there, looking out of the window, moonlight shining on her evil, sinister face. She vowed to find and destroy Tracie.

EVELLIA

CHAPTER 4
COURAGE

As it turned out, Tracie and Kibble walked through the night and the next morning. She had an idea where she was going but this was the first time she had been this way on foot. She was always in a car when she rode this part of town. She walked all the way through the park and into one of the busiest streets in Philly. Ridge Avenue. Ridge Avenue was like a big market place. That's where everybody came to buy their groceries and meats and fruits. The street was alive with people bustling about. She could hear the sounds of chickens and pigs and peoples voices. There was a lot of people out there and she and Kibble were among them.

She could see the clock on top of the church steeple ahead. It was almost seven o'clock. She was very hungry and cold. She just didn't know how she was going to eat or where she was going to stay. She had no money and she knew no one so she decided to sit on a crate next to one of the vendor's tables. As she sat and watched the activities, she was approached by an older woman. The woman seemed nice enough. She offered her some fruit and a drink of juice but the woman kept walking as she offered the great looking food and drink. Tracie saw that the woman was heading up into an alley and down some steps. Frightened, though she was, she was more hungry and cold. So she followed the old lady up into the alley and down the steps. Once down the steps, she found herself in a room, sort of.

It was dark except for a fire that was in a can outside the door. She could see other people were in there. The place had an odd smell. Other than that, it was okay. The old woman walked to the back of the place and came back with two oranges, an apple and a cup of apple juice. Tracie wasted no time gulping the juice and peeling the orange. She was invited to sit down and get warm. Tracie sat down on an empty crate. She finished the orange in no time flat and was now biting into the apple. She happened to look up and see a man. He had sat up on the floor and was staring at her. He had no teeth in his mouth and he looked like his breath didn't smell good. His clothes were tattered and dirty. The old lady had disappeared and Tracie was clutching Kibble in her arms and looking around for her. When she failed to locate her in a few minutes she decided to get out of there. She dashed out of the little cove and ran up the alley and back onto the street.

It was beginning to get dark and Tracie and her little puppy still had not figured out what they were doing. They walked and stopped and walked some more. Finally, they happened upon the park. The park was on the edge of the city and they just wandered on into it, headed for what they thought was an abandoned property. The building wasn't too far into the park yet it wasn't quite visible from the street. It was a rather shabby looking piece of real estate but, nonetheless, appealing to these two visitors. It stood alone. It was at least three stories high and it was almost shaped like a huge barn. The windows on the side of the property had been boarded up with plywood and tin.

The front of the house still retained a portion of pavement and the original marble steps with the little iron thing people used to use to clean the mud off of their boots.

Tracie and her friend ventured closer to the house. Not knowing what to expect or what they would do once there. They approached the steps with caution. The first thing she noticed was that the door was not boarded up and it was slightly ajar. Cautiously, Tracie tipped up the steps and peeped inside. She saw nothing but darkness.

"Hellooooo!" Tracie yelled. She waited. But no one answered. "What do you think, Kibble? Doesn't look like anybody lives here. Lets be brave and go in. Maybe we can stay here for a while. She boldly took a step inside, gently pushing the door open. She felt for a light switch, miraculously, she found it and turned it on. Surprised that the light switch worked, she stopped dead in her tracks. Her eyes became as wide as saucers as she scanned the house. Satisfied that no one else was in there with them, she stepped all the way in and stood very still.

"Hmmmm, nobody here." she said again. "Hellooooo!" Is anybody here?" She called out much louder than the first time. Her confidence was getting stronger and she sensed that she wouldn't get an answer. She didn't. She began to feel a little more comfortable now and slowly began to make her way through the vestibule and into the living room. She was amazed at what she was seeing. The place actually looked as if someone lived there.

There was a table, chairs, and a fireplace that had cinders in it. There was a lamp and an ashtray and books and magazines and paper. In general, the place was very untidy and it smelled like somebody's stinky feet. She ventured past the living room into the dining area which was connected to the kitchen. There was a string attached to the light that hung over the dining room table. She pulled the string and the light popped on. Roaches scattered everywhere. She jumped back and immediately began looking around her feet making sure they didn't jump on her. It made her itch. She was definitely not accustomed to being around these little creatures.

The table was disgusting. There was seven chairs placed around it and all of them appeared to have been eaten from because there was food in each of the chairs. There were seven plates, one in front of each chair. They all were filthy and they had food stuck to them. It was clear that no one washed the dishes in this place. The glasses were dirty and stained. Some were still half filled with whatever it was they had been drinking. Bottles and bags and silverware were haphazardly strewn about on the table. It was a big mess. She merely peered into the kitchen area and noticed that the sink also was filled with dirty dishes and glasses.

Eeeww!" was all she said. "Who could live like this?" Tracie was truly disgusted with the layout and she didn't know whether to leave of stay. After a second of thought, she decided to stay. At least it wasn't as cold in there as it was outside.

And there was light. Looking about her, she noted that she was also right at the base of the steps leading to the upstairs. Curious as to what that could look like, she turned on the light- switch. From the bottom of the stairs she could see the hallway and the top of the steps there was a door. She slowly began to go up the steps. Upon reaching the top she was amused at what she saw. Aside from the awful smell, it wasn't that bad. There were four rooms and each room had a wooden name plate hanging on the door.

She walked up to the closest room and read the name plate. "HONEY," it read. The door was shut but she opened it ever so slightly and peeped her head in. The room was spotless. Painted pink and red. It's bed was covered with a bedspread embroidered with red roses. The bed was as neatly made as ever a bed could be neatly made and there were shoes under it. They looked like women's shoes. Strange, though it seemed to her, they were in a perfect line. She peeped into the closet and there was also women's clothes hanging in there. She figured that a woman must sleep in this room. She backed out of the room careful not to disturb anything on the way out. She closed the door and turned to the next room.

"SCOOTA" the sign read. The door was opened enough so that she could easily peep in. The room was sort of neat but cluttered with records and posters.

She identified a strobe light and the walls that were painted in day glow paint. There was a red bulb in the light socket and it smelled of some sort of incense.

She backed out of that room and looked into the next door. "MONEY", was the name on this sign. She opened the door and stepped in. The bed was not made up but the clothes were in order and shoes in place. A few decks of playing cards and dice and gambling devices were in plain view. There was a wad of money on the dresser and some jewelry. That may come in handy, she thought. The next room was marked "STUTTER".

She smiled as she thought about the names. "What funny names these people have. Don't you think so Kibble?" The dog didn't answer. "I'll bet these are the children's room, and their parents sleep in that room marked Honey!"

She was quite pleased to come to that conclusion. She felt better knowing that she would be among a family when they finally returned from wherever they were. She had begun to suspect that they would be back. Stutter's room wasn't so bad either, so she just looked in and saw men's clothes and a small radio and the bed. The last room was at the base of yet another flight of steps that led to a third floor. She always thought a third floor of a house was spooky. This caused her to think twice about going up there but after she turned on the light and looked for a minute, she got up the courage and went. Cautiously!

At the top of the stairs she saw that there were only three rooms and they too were adorned with name plates on the doors. The smell was overpowering and was apparently the source of the smell that went all through the house. She held her nose closed with two fingers and waved her hand in front of her. She was standing in front of the room at the very top of the stairs. The name was "FUNKY". Tracie quickly moved on to the door across from it.

"Whew!" she exclaimed as she looked at the door. "CHUNKY" was the name on this tag. Looking in, she saw that the room was littered with potato chip and pretzel bags and pop sickle sticks and soda bottles...it was a mess. She just closed the door and looked at the last room which had "POOTA" hanging on the door. This room was in the farthest corner of the house and sort of sat by itself. She went to it and opened the door. There was a faint smell of some potent gas but not so bad that she had to back off. She just peeped in from the outside.

She saw many Pepto Bismo and Maalox bottles and medicine capsules. That was enough for her. She went back down the stairs suddenly realizing that she was really tired and sleepy. She had not slept since she left the hospital. That was a long time ago. So, she decided to take a nap. She chose the room marked Honey to do it in. She went in and left the door open so she could hear if anyone came home. She fell fast asleep.

CHAPTER 5

EVELLIA'S EVIL PLAN

Meanwhile, back at Tracie's old house, Evellia occupied her time prancing around teasing her hair and fixing her clothes on her tall, skinny body. She, of course, continued to admire herself in every mirror she laid her eyes on. She seemed to be in good spirits as she underwent her daily rituals. Even though she had been obsessed with getting young Tracie, she was content to wait. She had already figured out what she had concluded to be the best way to do it, and not have herself involved. She decided to hire somebody to do it for her. And that's what she did. She hired two hench men who were scheduled to arrive there any minute. It was about three o'clock in the afternoon yet she still had candles burning everywhere. The house was dark and ugly as she only allowed a minimum of sunlight to filter in through the heavy drapes that covered the windows. The doorbell rang. It distracted Evellia from her self admiration festival. She became very angry. She always became angry when anything pulled her away from herself.

"Who the heck is that? She bellowed. "If you touch that bell again I'll snap your fingers off one by one. "She stomped over to the door and snatched it open. Outside, standing huddled together, were two men.

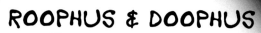

ROOPHUS & DOOPHUS

One was very tall and muscular and the other was very short and skinny. The taller man was dressed in a tan raincoat and was wearing a big hat that covered his eyes. He was looking down on Evellia. The smaller one was dressed in a gray overcoat and was wearing a black wide brim hat. He was looking up at Evellia. Squinting and sneering, she looked up at the taller man and down at the smaller man before growling.

"Who the heck are you idiots? I know you're not who I think you are? Are you?" she asked. She clearly was not pleased with what she saw. She was expecting two henchmen and she didn't expect them to look like they did.

The small guy spoke up first. "Pardon me Miss but we s'posed to meet with a, wait a minute, (he unfolded a piece of paper he had balled up in his hand and held it close to his face to read from it) uh, a Miss Evans. Yeah. Ms. Evelyn Evans. Is she here?"

"It's Evellia. E-V-E-L-L-I-A Evellia, not Evelyn you moron. Who are you? Are you the jerks I hired to do a job?"

"At your service, ma'am? Right Doo?", the shorter one replied.

"Uh, yeah bawth." The taller man was grinning all the while, exposing the fact that he had one tooth missing in the front row of his upper teeth and one missing in the front row of his lower set of teeth. He "thpoke with a lithp". He looked really stupid.

Evellia almost wanted to laugh but she restrained herself and remained her regular old irritable self instead.

After sizing them up one more time, she pushed open the door and snarled, "Well shut up and get in here. And you better not break nothing on the way in you goof-balls. You hear me?"

"Uh, yeah, Doo, be careful walking in."

"Uh. Ok bawth." and he began to tippytoe through the house smiling his hideous smile.

As it turned out, the smaller man's name was Roofus, he was the leader of the two. And the taller man's name was Doophus, he did the actual work.

Evellia kept an eye on them both as she ushered them into the kitchen.

"Did anybody see you come up here?", she asked suspiciously.

"No. Nobody saw us! Don't worry about that. We was real careful to see that we just acted naturally. Right Doo?" He always seemed to have to confer with the taller man after saying something.

"Uh. Yeah bawth." The same hideous grin spread across his face as he answered.

"Ok. Ok. Did you find out anything? Where is she? What?? Tell me, I must know."

Evellia was anxious to know if the hired hit men had found out any information as to the whereabouts of her stepsister, Tracie.

"Ok. Uh, see, it's like this, see. We heard on the streets that a girl and a dog was spotted on the Ridge. That's Ridge Avenue, you know! And she, um, was seen walking around down there. Right Doo?" Roophus answered. And of course Doophus had his usual answer.

"Uh. Yeah bawth." And of course he did the grin. He seemed proud of himself that he could even say that much. Evellia looked bewildered as to how someone could be so big and stupid. She was amazed.

"Well. What else? What else?" Evellia prodded.

"Oh. And like they was walking along and like, Lillian, the bag broad was wit' em. Right Doo?"

"Uh. Yeah bawth." Evellia felt they weren't talking fast enough or giving enough information. She began to grow intolerant.

"Look you idiots. I don't have time to be messin' around. Where is she now? You hear me? Now? Where is that little thief? I WANT TO KNOW! NOW!" Her voice had risen to a very high pitch and was very loud. Both men were almost cowering as she fussed at them.

"I-I-I-I-I;m tellin' you. I'm tellin' you NOW. At least I'm tryin' to tell you but...uh, wait a minute. Is you payin' us for this?"

Roophus had just then remembered that he was supposed to say that first.

" 'Cause we need gas money and stuff. And...
" Evellia snapped back at him.

"Ohhhhhhh. You fool. You idiot. Yes, yes, yes, yes I'll pay you." She reached her hand down the front of her dress and brought out a one hundred dollar bill and handed it to Roophus. "There...you money grubbing little doo doo. Take it and go get your gas and whatever else you need. Just tell me where that little criminal is. Do you hear me? Tell me?"

Roophus began inspecting the bill by holding it up to the light and tugging at both ends.

"Ok. Now. See, it's like this, see, Lillian, the bag broad, saw her head for the park. And the only place down that way is where the little guys live. And that's where we thinks she's stayin'. We thinks she livin' wit' em. Right Doo?"

"Uh. Yeah bawth."

"Little guys?", Evellia snapped, "Lit...what are you telling me? That she's staying with a bunch of little people? Who are these people? And why are they little? What are they doing with her? They better not kill her or I'll kill them. I swear, I'll kill them so help me...never mind, never mind. Listen to me you two feeble minded males. And listen well. I will give you five thousand dollars. *Minus* the one hundred dollars I just gave you. So that would be four thousand nine hundred dollars if you find her and bring her back to me. Dead or alive."

"If she's not already dead, that is. But you must bring her body back to me before I give you one red cent. Do you understand me? You must bring me her body. I must see it."

"Five thousand dollars? Oooooowee! For five G's we'll ice her and bring her back on the bus, if we have to. Right Doo?" This seemed to be an awful lot of money to Roophus and he was, indeed, excited. Doophus, on the other hand, didn't seem to notice.

"Uh. Yeah bawth."

"Fine! Now get on out of here and do what you got to do. No. No. Wait a minute!" Evellia, apparently thought better of leaving it up to them to decide on the method they would use to do the job, so she asked, "I want to know just how you plan to do it!"

"Do what? Get her on the bus? Oh that's easy. See, we'll..."

Evellia almost knocked his head off, she hit him so hard. His head toppled to the side and his hat flew off of his head and landed in the dinning room under the table.

"NO! NO! NO! Stupid. I mean *get rid of her.* How are you going to do it! What? Shoot her? Stab her? Blow her up? What? How?" She was really angry at their stupidity. And he was once again cowering. Doophus had stepped back equally as afraid.

"Uh. Oh, oh, I see what you mean now." Roophus began talking as he looked for his hat because he had a bald head and was insecure without his hat on his head. Looking frantically around, he spotted it lying on the floor under the table.

"Get my skimmer for me Doo!", he directed to Doophus. "Uh, sure bawth." Doo replied. Evellia was seething as she looked at the two discussing the hat. Doophus saw her anger and stopped in his tracks. He was shaking as he stood there looking at her.

"Stop standin' there with that stupid look on your face and go on in there and get my hat." Roophus told him again.

"Uh. Where bawth?" Doophus couldn't take his eyes off of Evellia. Roophus reached up and snatched his head in the direction of his hat and pushed him toward it. He followed him into the dining room walking past Evellia.

"I'm waiting!", Evellia sternly reminded them.

As Doophus bent over to get the hat, he was at ear level with Roophus who had pulled his ear to him and whispered something in his ear. Doophus looked up at him and grinned. They both seemed pleased and they headed back to the kitchen.

"Ok. See, it's like this, see. We figure that she's gonna have to come out soon, see. And when she does, we'll be in the van. See, we got this bad Volkswagen Van see. And we'll be in the van and when she come out, we gone see her and we gone follow her and at the right time...BAM. We just gone run her over."

"Then, see, we gone get out and pick her up like we was takin' her to the hospital, but really what we gone do is put her in the back of the van and bring her back here instead. We collect our five G's and we gone. How's that sound? Pretty good, huh? Sound good to us. Right Doo?

"Uh. Yeah bawth." Doophus doesn't grin this time. He grimaced and scratched the side of his head as if he were baffled by the plan. Evellia was not impressed.

"Fine! Ok. Whatever. Now get out of here and find her and do it. I don't want to see either of your stupid faces till you have her here in front of me...dead or alive. Do you hear me...DEAD OR ALIVE!"

CHAPTER 6
THE EVIL PLAN GOES WRONG

Meanwhile, back at the house in the park, Tracie awoke from her nap and decided to help the family out by cleaning the house for them. She began by sweeping the front of the house. It wasn't that cold outside so she even scrubbed the marble steps until they were as white as the snow. Then, she went into the house and cleaned. Which was quite a task! From the vestibule to the kitchen.

When she finally finished, it was about four o'clock in the afternoon and she was hungry. She didn't have any money, but she remembered a wad of money in one of the rooms upstairs so, she went upstairs and found the money in Money's room. She took a twenty dollar bill from the wad. She didn't think they would mind if she bought food for them, because their cupboards were bare. She decided to go to Ridge Avenue where she remembered she first entered the city. Picking up little Kibble, she started for the Avenue. Ever so cautious as she stepped out of the house, she immediately noticed a green Volkswagon van slowly pulling off behind her. She suspected it may be following her but she continued on to the market along the Ridge where she stopped and bought some bread, meat, potatoes and mayonnaise, etc. and started back to the house. She again noticed the green van and the first chance she got, she ducked out of sight into a little alley.

As she was hiding, the van cruised past her.

Little did the criminals in the van know that they were about to make a very costly mistake. There happened to be another person in the area that was dressed very similar to Tracie. Same pants and jacket. After circling the block a few times in search of Tracie, Roophus and Doophus spotted this person from afar. Sure that they had found Tracie they began to put their plan into effect.

"There she is. I knew she couldn't of got away. I got her now. Hold on Doo. I'm gonna do her now. Hold on."

They sped toward the person they suspected to be Tracie and...POW... they plowed into the unsuspecting soul. The body flew a few feet into the air and landed right in front of the van. People were screaming and running to give aid. But Roophus was first out of the van and was pretending to administer first aid to her as if he really cared. She was obviously dead, he thought. The body lay twisted and mangled and the face had been smashed beyond recognition. There was one other thing that was also obvious. It was not a girl. It was a boy. And Roophus knew that little Tracie was not a boy. Doophus also leaned over him to act as though he were helping the unfortunate victim. Roophus noticed the difference immediately.

"Oh boy Doo". There was panic in his voice. "This ain't the same one we been following. I don't know Doo. This could be a problem. What we gone do, Doo?"

"Uh. I don't know bawth."

"Well, I got an idea. Stop standin' there lookin' stupid and gimme' a hand puttin' her, I mean him in the van." They struggled with the heavy body and finally succeeded in convincing the bystanders that they were taking the body to the hospital as they lifted it into the back of the van. Once it was in the van and secured, Roophus and Doophus hurriedly got in and sped away. Off they went in the pea green Volkswagen van.

"Ok. Now you got to listen Doo. I got a plan. This is what we gone do. Ok Doo?"

"Uh. Ok bawth."

"Ok. See, now what we gone do is this. We are gonna act like this is really her. You know! The one we been followin. Right? And we gone take her to that mean lady's house at night. Right? See, 'cause in the dark, she ain't gone be able to see that good. Right? And we gone act just like it's her. We gone get paid! Right? And then we gone get outta there real fast. Right? Got that Doo?" Doophus, of course, didn't even understand what Roophus was talking about, but he answered anyway.

"Uh. Yeah bawth."

The van eventually stalled some distance from the house, so they decided to carry it up the hill. When they finally reached the house, Evellia was waiting at the door. As usual, she was angry. Steam was rising from her hair.

"What took you so long?", she said calmly. Then in the same breath, she screamed at them. "Get in here".

As they scrambled to enter, Doophus bumped his head on the light fixture, causing it to break. They were in darkness. Evellia barked at them for a while before kneeling down in an effort to identify the body by the light of the moon. The garage door was left open at the bottom. The moonlight shone under it but It was not enough light to see very good.

As it were, the victim's face had been so badly injured that she really didn't, nor could she, make a proper identification.

"Are you sure that 's her? I can't really see since that jerk broke the light."

"Oh yeah. Oh yeah! It's her all right. Yeah, it's basically her. Trust me! We did every thing right, Miss Evans. Now we just wants to get paid and we gon' be gone. You got the money?" Evellia was just a little suspicious as to why Roophus was in such a rush to get the money she had promised them.

"Oh wait a minute." Evellia directed to them. She was not to be rushed.

She continued trying to see the face but in the dim light, it was impossible. She got up off her knees and headed up the stairs. Not really satisfied but content, for now, to at least have a body that was said to be that of young Tracie.

"I'm going to get your money. While I'm gone, you two put the body in that big box over there in the corner and I'll dispose of it later." She disappeared up the steps and Roophus and Doophus quickly moved to do as they have been directed. But as they attempted to move the box, it toppled over and the body rolled out of the box and under the door and down the steep hill. Roophus and Doophus tried to stpo it but they couldn't. Just looked as it disappeared in the snowy darkness. They looked at each other then to the opened space then they moved quickly to the box. They picked up the empty box and put it in the corner. Just then, Evellia called to them and they came up the stairs as if nothing had happened. She looked at them very strangely as she handed Roophus a stack of bills, which he never even bothered to count. Roohpus tried not to look at her as they both turned and headed for the door as fast as they could. Never saying a word. Out the door they went. They ran down the hill where the van had stalled. Slipping and sliding they managed to reach the van and get in. Luckily, they were able to get it started. The van began to swerve and slide back down the hill and they made their exit. Not a word was spoken between the two.

Evellia was glad to see them leave. She relaxed and calmly, she
gazed into the mirror, smiling at her image, then, she looked up the
steps. She had Maureen in mind. After admiring herself in all of her
mirrors. And after assuring herself that little Tracie was out of the
way she figured that all of her troubles were over.

   "Maureen dear," she called in a most soothing voice, "can we
talk?"

   "Of course Evellia. Your wish is my command." Maureen
always responded in a trance-like voice.

   "Good. Now bring out those cards and let's see what they
have to say." Maureen already had the deck stacked in front of her.
Evellia came into the room and knelt down in front of Maureen. The
cards were between them. Then Maureen began to chant.

> *AT YOUR REQUEST I'LL DO MY BEST*
> *TO PUT YOUR HOPES AND FEARS TO REST*
> *THE CARDS WILL TELL IF ALL IS WELL*
> *FOR THEY RELEASE THE MYSTERIES OF*
> *HEAVEN AND HELL*

   Maureen sighed deeply after the chant and fell into
a trance. The cards began to mysteriously shuffle and deal themselves. After they were finished, a loud tone sounded out of the air.

MAUREEN

"What do they say? Come on. Come on. What?"
Evellia leaned over the cards to grab Maureen by her shoulders. Shaking her violently. Maureen's head was being rattled from side to side when suddenly, her eyes popped open. Only the whites could be seen. She spoke.

AN EVIL DEED'S BEEN TRIED AND FAILED
A SOUL'S BEEN TAKEN BUT TRUE SOUL PREVAILS
ONE TRUTHFUL AND PURE AND DIVINE IN SPIRIT
ALAS, YOU EVELLIA, ARE NOWHERE NEAR IT.

Upon hearing these words, Evellia flew into a rage. She slapped the cards out of sequence and scattered them about the room. She then slapped Maureen and cursed her.

"Get out of here you fake." she yelled at the top of her voice, "You don't know what you're saying. Get out of here. Now." Her voice could be heard for miles. She forcefully pushed and kicked her out of the room and down the steps. She followed swiftly and continued her murderous attack on the helpless woman rolling her along with her foot until she was at the threshold of the door. Then with one movement, she opened the door and rolled her out of it and into the snowy cold. After ejecting Maureen into the cold she ran back upstairs and threw the cards out of the window. In her frenzy, she had become completely unraveled. Her clothes were disheveled and rearranged on her thin torso. She looked haggard and old with the gray strands of her hair standing apart from the bluish hairs. She caught a glimpse of herself in the mirror. She was appalled at what she saw.

Her ugly personality, somehow, had emerged in her appearance and she was ugly and wrinkled. Her face even seemed to change shape. She looked like an old witch. As she stared at the image in the mirror her eyes gradually allowed her to see something else. In her evil, twisted mind, instead of seeing ugly, she was looking at a young beautiful face. The one she once had. This made her feel better. Although her true image was that of an old, wrinkled, ugly woman, she believed she was still beautiful. She smiled to herself and attempted to regain her composure. As she did so, another thought entered her mind. Tracie's body.

She recalled the events of the evening and decided to get a light and go down in the basement to get and even closer look at the body in the box. For some reason she just was not totally satisfied with what she saw. She began to wonder if she had been duped. Once in the basement, she went directly to the box and shone the light on the body. She opened the box. It was empty...

Evellia began to breathe heavily. Steam once again rose from her body. She was livid beyond words. She couldn't even stand up she was so mad. She just fell to the floor and sat there...steaming. She began to think. Think out loud. As she did so, a strange peace came over her ugly face. She rubbed her hands together the way a fly does before he eats his food. She kept her eyes fixed on the darkness around her.

"Ok boys. Fine! You couldn't do it. Fine! I'll just have to do it myself. I'll get that little wench myself. I know what, she smiled insanely at her plan, I'll go to Baltimore, yes, that's what I'll do. I'll go to Baltimore, and I'll get Cassandra. No, better yet, I'll get Lenora. Yes. Lenora, the High Priestess of Darkness. She will aid me. Yes, that's what I'll do. I'll leave tomorrow."

Evellia was very pleased with her new devious plan. She gathered he composure and began to make preparation to leave for Baltimore on the first train leaving Philadelphia. She was now obsessed with relieving Tracie of her life...and her inheritance.

CHAPTER 7
HELP ARRIVES

As Tracie slept on the sofa, she managed to curl herself into a little ball under the covers. For a little girl, she snored like an old man. She was snoring and making strange sounds as she slumbered.

Outside the house a truck pulled up. It was an old, raggedy pickup truck loaded down with dirt and dirty tools and seven men. The men were not of average height. As a matter of fact they were very small. They were weary, tired, and sleepy.

As they climbed out of the truck and began removing their tools they were too weary to notice how clean the windows were on the house or how white the marble steps were. They lived there but they had not been there for a few weeks. They had been in Delaware County where they had been under contract doing construction work. They had been gone for weeks and had now happily completed their work. They just wanted to rest when all of a sudden one of them noticed how clean the front of the house was. He held up his hand signaling the rest of them to stop.

"Holeup, yall.", said the one called Scoota, "Somethin's wrong here. This place ain't never been this clean. Look! What happened to all the trash and stuff that used to be over there? And look! Look at the steps. They actually white. Somethin' ain't right!"

They all stopped what they are doing and looked around at one another. Slowly, they continued taking the picks, axes, and shovels off the truck. They started toward the house. The one called Money was leading the crew. He stopped and held his hands up in the air.

"Hold it. I don't like it. What if somebody in there? Look. The door ain't even shut all the way." He looked around at the crew and settled his eyes on Scoota. Scoota was the taller of the seven.

"Why don't you go on in there and make sure everything okay, Scoota?"

"Why me? Why I got to be the one? Why can't we all go?" Scoota asked, defiantly.

" 'Cause! You the one that saw it first. That's why. And anyway, if all us go, who gone stand guard? Now go on in there. You ain't scared, is you, boy?" Money had a way of assuming the leadership position with his logic and quick wit. Everybody else usually just followed his lead. They all looked at Scoota.

"Uh. No. No I ain't scared. Okay. I'll go, but if y'all hear anything. I mean anything. Y'all better come in there quick and help me."

"Aw don't worry about that, we'll be in there before they can get one lick in on you." said the one they call Chunky, the fat one.

Scoota collected himself and proceeded, with much skepticism, into the house.

Slowly, pushing open the door, he entered the vestibule. He saw his shadow and shrieked. He was carrying a shovel in his hand, holding it above his head as he crept ever so slowly inward. He barely got inside when he heard Tracie's snore. He immediately turned and bolted out of the house running into the arms of Chunky who they had pushed in front.

"They in there", he screamed, "they in there. I heard 'em". Breathing heavily, his eyes looked as though they were about to bulge out of their sockets. He continued to babble.

"Shut up, boy. Calm down. Now calm down. Dag! What you see?" Money attempted to make some sense of Scoota's babbeling.

"No. No I didn't *see* nothing. I *heard* 'em. They went like this." He made a ghostly sound. "Like that." He made the ghostly sound again. Money slapped him on the back of his head.

"Shut up. Okay, okay. Now listen up. This is what we gone do. We each got a weapon in our hands, right? So we'll all go in this time. And we'll attack it from all sides. Now everybody get something in your hands and get ready. Okay. Chunk, you the biggest so you go first." Chunky seemed not to mind. He fell in line first and everybody lined up behind him. Scoota and Money were jockeying for last place.

As they entered, they began tripping over one another while attempting to be as quiet as possible.

One was just as afraid as the other. Further, they crept into the house. They heard the snoring and strange sounds but they persevered and kept moving forward. As they came upon the sofa, Tracie was on the verge of awakening. Just at that moment, she sat straight up with the cover still over her head, and yawned, while at the same time, stretching her arms out from under the cover. The silhouette in the dark gave the illusion of something terrifying about to pounce on them. In unison, they all screamed and scattered throughout the house. Tools flew everywhere. Tracie screamed as well and jumped behind the sofa with Kibble close by her side. It was suddenly very quiet. After a couple of seconds, Tracie peeked out from behind the sofa and spoke.

"Please, please don't hurt me. I'll leave. I didn't mean to scare anyone. I-I-I just fell asleep." Tracie was most humble as she attempted to apologize for her intrusion.

One by one their little heads began to appear. Slowly, they emerged from their hiding places. They stared, in awe at the lovely young figure standing before them. Money, instinctively reached for the lights so he could better see what so frightened them. But it was Tracie who was amazed at what she now could plainly see in the light.

"Oh my goodness", she exclaimed, "You're not children at all. You're dwarfs", Tracie said in high pitched voice. But being referred to as dwarfs upset them to such a degree that Stutter chimed up.

W-w-w-w-e ain't no d-d-d-d-d-warfs." Stutter retorted adamantly.

"Shut up, boy", said Money, Then he turned and looked at tracie.

"We ain't no dwarfs, little girl. We little people. But never mind that. Just who are you? And what you doing here?", Money demanded.

"Hold up." Yet another voice was heard from.

"I ain't no dwarf an I ain't no little person! I'm just as big as you. Look." Scoota sidled up to the young lady to show that he was at least as tall as she was. He was! Admittedly, he was somewhat small in stature, but the fact remained that he was slightly taller than the other six people in the room. Just as he started to walk, Pootas' voice distracted him.

"S'cuse me."

At that, his eyes opened wide as saucers, he pushed the little girl out of his way, opened the window and jumped out.

Upon hearing this, everyone, except Tracie and Poota, dashed for the doors and the windows.

Shortly thereafter, Tracie grimaced and grabbed her nose. The air had been tainted with an unpleasant smell. She began fanning her hands frantically in disbelief. After a moment they cautiously drifted back in, only to find Tracie talking to Poota.

"You have got to be the one they call Poota. Right?", she said to him. Before he could answer, Money began chastising him.

"Why you do that Poota? Why did you have to wait 'til we got inside to do that?" Money inquired of him. "My god boy. Don't you have no home trainin'?" Poota lowered his head in shame.

"I'm sorry. I tried to hold it in but it just got loose and...hey. Hey, did y'all hear that? She called my name. Y'all hear that? She knows my name." Poota was all smiles. But Money glared at the girl with suspicion.

"She musta' been snoopin around upstairs and seen the names on the doors, stupid. Ain't you?" He pointed first to Poota then to Tracie. Then, out of habit, he pulled out a small wad of money and began to thumb through it as if he were counting it. By now Tracie was amused and smiling as she looked at them one at a time.

"And you? You must be Money!", she said as she pointed in his direction. " And you must be the one called Chunky", she said, changing the direction of her eyes to the overweight figure. Then she looked at the one in pink pants and a "not-so-very-masculine" hat.

"You must be Honey. I can tell by the way you're dressed. Oh, and that's a nice hat you're wearing." The group turned their attention to Honey and Tracie returned her attention to them.

"And I know you are Stutter, because I heard you talk, and you, you must be Scoota. And Lord knows you are the Poota." She said, pointing in Poota's direction.

At this point, everyone was relaxed and a little more comfortable with Tracie. And she, with them.

"Y-y-y-y-y-y-you're b-b-b-b-b-beautiful." exclaimed Stutter.

"Now just hold on there Stuts", Scoota chimed in,...as a matter of fact", he turned his attention to Tracie, and in his most charming voice, said to her, "My name is Scoota and they call me that because when I was little, uh, I mean when I was a boy I used to always ride a scooter. Now, may I have the pleasure of knowing your name?" Scoota attempted to be very cordial and mannerly as he spoke.

"Oh. I'm sorry. My name is Tracie. Tracie Phillips. And this is my puppy, Kibble. Say hi Kibble." she jokingly said to the little puppy. The puppy said nothing.

"Well, young lady," Money said, "Uh, I mean, Tracie, that's all well and good but, just what *are* you doing in our house?" With that, he folded his arms in front of him, tapped his foot nervously on the floor and peered into Tracie's eyes.

Tracie sat down on the sofa and commenced to talk. She began to tell them the whole story. How her parents were killed in the accident; how Evellia took over. How she fled and now felt that Evellia was after her. The whole story, up to and including how she ended up on the sofa that very night.

The story took a very long time to tell and by then, everyone was sitting around her listening with sympathetic ears. When she finally finished, Money was the first one to make a comment.

"Hmmm", he uttered thoughtfully, "that's a big problem you got there, girlie. Let me ask you this. Do you think your, uh, stepsister knows you're here?"

They all looked to Tracie for her answer.

"Oh. I don't know. I just don't know. I really *hope* *s*he doesn't but I just can't say for sure. Look. All I'm asking is if you will allow me to stay here for just a little while, I would be ever so grateful. Besides, I could cook and clean for you. I could be like your "live-in maid." Tracie was sincere and convincing as she spoke and the looks on the faces of the little men indicated that they were giving serious thought to her proposal.

"No problem. We can help you" said Scoota.

At that moment, Honey interrupted and said, "That's right, deary and you would be welcome to stay in my room.

She put her arm around Tracie's shoulders. She then looked at Tracie up close and could see that she was as yet a child in her teens. Although she had the face of an ebony angel, she was not that big for her age.

"Just how old are you, sweety?", Honey inquired. She was a little leery as to Tracie's age, due to her small size.

"Seventeen!", Tracie happily revealed, " I just turned seventeen. That's when I got Kibble."

Honey was convinced.

"Now you just come on with me sweety."

She took hold of Tracie's hand and lead her up the stairs to her room and closed the door. The little men were left standing to mumble and grumble among themselves.

"Ok. So now, she's just a little girl and we have to protect her. It's our duty to look after our children. I don't want to hear of nobody sayin' nothin' out of the way to nobody. Y'all hear me." Money respectfully admonished each one of them with these words of advice. And they all agreed to protect and care for her. They all felt the same way. She needed their help.

In the meantime, Tracie reopened Honey's door and called down the steps in a playful tone.

"I hope you guys noticed that I cleaned up the house...including that filthy kitchen. I didn't get a chance to do your rooms but I will get around to them tomorrow. Oh! And before we go to bed, I don't think I'll be able to tolerate these smells. So If you all could just be mindful of that I would appreciate it. Now goodnight."

She closed the door and the little men began to smell themselves as they continued to mumble and grumble. Just then they heard Poota.

"S'cuse me!" Again, they broke for the nearest exit, cursing and screaming at Poota as they ran for fresh air.

Poota just stood there, in the middle of the floor.

CHAPTER 8
TRACIE LEFT ALONE

Tracie and the little people were getting along just magnificently. Two weeks had gone by since they met. They were having a great time. The group sort of adopted Tracie and treated her as though she were their little sister. They took her out on the town. And to the various Theaters and Concerts that were in town. To the movies, the circus, she was having a glorious time.

One morning, Chunky left out to go to the mail box which was pretty far away from the house, nearby the road.

When he came back, it was with some good news and some bad news.

"Hey fellas, there was some mail in the box and it's good news. Listen."

They gathered around to hear him read the letter. The letter was sent to inform them of an inpending construction job back in Delaware. Furthermore, the job was to last approximately two to three weeks. They were all very happy because it was difficult to keep steady work these days. And they were almost out of food.

"Wow. Isn't that great. We was almost out of food." Chunky was particularly happy because he just loved to eat.

"And Toilet paper too", he added.

"Yeah, I guess so, the way you eat." Funky retorted. Funky very seldom said anything but he, too, had a penchant for food. So he kept an eye on Chunky and his eating habits.

Shooot. It's a wonder anything lasts two minutes in this house with your big butt around." All the while, Tracie was beginning to become aware of the reality of the up and coming situation.

"Does this mean that you guys will be gone for two or three weeks? You mean I'll be here by myself?" She was fearful and it was showing on her face. Honey immediately sensed her concern and moved closer to console her.

"Oh. Yeah. That's right. But baby you ain't got nothing to worry about. If that old bag ain't found you yet. She ain't gonna'. Believe me. Plus, you got the dog here to protect you. He won't let nothing happen to you. Right Kibble?" The dog said nothing.

"Just don't be goin' up on the avenue...and make sure the doors and windows are locked every night. You know what I mean? There ought to be enough food here to last you for two weeks. That is if we can get outta here before Chunkybutt starts gettin' hungry again."

Scoota also tried to allay Tracie's fears with a little humor; although Chunky didn't think it was so funny.

"Why y'all always got to blame me? I eat the same as y'all. I ain't the only one eatin' around here you know?" All the while he was leaning in the refrigerator as he spoke.

Then they heard the dreaded words of Poota.

S'cuse me."

Tracie looked at him with astonishment as she grabbed her nose.

"Aw Poota! I thought you said you'd go away from everybody when you felt a gas buildup!"

Then, she ran out the door with everyone else. Poota was left trying to explain.

"I'm sorry. I forgot." This time, he, himself, couldn't stand the odor and he ran out the door right along with everybody else.

Later that day they decided to have a little party to celebrate the good news. They went to the market and bought some party goods and put on some music. They danced and partied into the early morning hours. They had a great time. Tracie got a chance to dance with each one of them. Honey even tried to sneak in a dance or two. It was great.

The next afternoon, however, there was a tiny bit of sadness as they packed their tools and clothes onto the truck. They all, in their own way, assured Tracie that she was going to be safe. Then, the time came for them to leave. Tracie and Kibble waved them off and watched them ride out of the park and out of sight.

They sat on the steps for a while before going back into the house. When they did, it felt lonely. Tracie and Kibble were all alone in the big house.

CHAPTER 9
EVELLIA'S TRICKERY

That very same morning that the little people took off for their new job, Evellia arrived at Thirtieth Street Station. Just returning from her trip to Baltimore where she went to visit a "black magic woman" by the name of Lenora. She had successfully completed her mission which was to get some sort of potion or something evil that she could use to do away with her little stepsister, Tracie.

What she brought back with her was called "Zombie Powder". This powder, according to the black magic woman, could be used to make someone appear to be dead, when in reality, they actually were still alive. It was supposed to be able to slow down the pulse, heart rate and metabolism of the human body so much that even medical instruments could not take a reading. She was ecstatic about her plan. She hailed a taxi cab and was driven to her house where she immediately began to put her devious plan into effect. She admired herself as soon as she closed the door behind her and soon she was talking aloud to herself as she so often did. As there was seldom anyone else around for her to talk to.

"Oh no. I'm not going to waste another minute, no sirree. I'm going to start baking this apple pie right now. Oooooooeeee. It's going to look so inviting, so delicious, so scrumptious and good that it's even going to make my beautiful mouth water.

Ooooooeeee, I just love apple pie. But no! No- no-no-no Eviee. You mustn't be tempted. You must remember that this most delectable of pies will be spiced with Zombie Powder. And it is a very special pie for a very special, dirty, grubby, little worm of a person. Once I put this powerful most potent powder in the pie, I won't want any parts of it, to be sure. But *she* won't be able to resist it."

Evellia let loose a loud and wicked laugh. She then feverishly prepared the pie and put much Zombie Powder in it. She admired herself to the fullest as her pie was baking in the oven. When it was done, she marveled at it. It, indeed, was delectable and mouth watering. The crust was browned just right. It smelled heavenly. It was to die for.

"Ooooooo. My-o-my-o my. This is so tempting. Oh my goodness. I must remember to thank Lenora again. Her plan to give Zombie Powder to that little, ugly child was much better than mine. I would have just as soon slit her skinny little throat and drank her blood. But this Zombie Powder will make her appear to be dead and all the while, she will be alive, and that's just how she will be buried. *Alive.*" She again bellowed out the most horrible and wicked laughter. "ALIVE!" Her gruff voice amid the laughter resounded throughout the house. She became engrossed in her ill begotten success for a while, then, she continued with the second part of her plan which was to take care of the two bumbling killers. She had decided that she would disguise herself as an ugly, old woman and go out into the streets.

In the meantime, she had an idea just where Tracie could be found.

After pondering in the mirror for an hour or so, she called a taxicab and then she began trying to figure out just how she was going to turn all this beauty into ugly, she reasoned that it could be done, but only with enough make-up could she change her appearance entirely. One of Evellia's most outstanding features, aside from her large, broken nose, was a large mole on her chin. There was little she could do with that so she let it be. She worked on herself for a while, then, satisfied that she no longer looked like herself she put the luscious apple pie in a brown paper bag and carefully, ever so carefully, carried it out the door to a waiting taxicab.

Once in the city, she was dropped off near the park. She didn't know exactly where she was going but she knew to seek the bag lady named Lillian. She didn't have to wander very far before coming upon her. As she approached the bag lady, she forced tears to her eyes and assumed a look of distress.

"Pardon me deary. But I'm looking for my poor, lost little girl and her puppy. I understand they were seen along this road not long ago. Is there any way you could possibly help me?" She had a gleam in her eye as she awaited a response from the bag lady.

"Excuse me?", the lady replied, "No! I ain't seen no"...

At that moment, the old lady produced a one hundred dollar bill and made sure Lillian saw it.

"Uh, wait a minute, ya' know? She quickly grabbed the one hundred dollar bill that the old lady was dangling in front of her face and held it tight in her hand.

"I didn't think no more about it but, yeah. I did see 'em a couple days ago. I was tryin' to take care of 'em but they disappeared on me. Ya' know? I think I heard somebody say they saw 'em headed down to the park. I don't know for sure, old woman, but you may want to try the old house that's standin' not to far off of Thirty-Third Street. Down there a ways." Lillian pointed the old lady in the direction of the house.

"Thank you kindly. I am ever so grateful for you help. Bye now." As she departed company with the bag lady she was over heard to whisper.

"You just don't know *how* grateful, you stupid old bag.!" And she hastily moved toward the park.

Tracie and Kibble were curled up on the sofa listening to records and watching the little TV set in the living room. It was peaceful and quiet. Suddenly, Kibble became restless. He jumped from the couch, sniffing, pacing back and forth from the back door to the sofa. Tracie became uneasy with this change in his behavior and she too went on alert.

"What's the matter Kibble? What is it? Is there something wrong?" Tracie was concerned, because she had never known the dog to act like that and she was getting scared. She looked around the house but didn't see anything visibly wrong. Getting up, she went to the window. She opened it and peeped her head up and down in the direction of the street.

"I don't see anything out here, Kibble. I think you just may be a little on edge because our new found friends are not here."

Satisfied that there was nothing that she could see, she closed the window but as she turned around, she was aghast to find an old woman standing in the dining room.

"Ahhhhhh!" she shrieked. She was so terrified she could do nothing but scream.

The old lady stepped toward her in a gesture meant to console her but Tracie stepped out of reach and fell onto the couch.

"My goodness! Forgive me! I didn't mean to frighten you deary, but, uh, your back door was open and, uh, you see, I thought this was the home of one of my dear friends."

The air was cold and there was a cold, evil gleam in the old woman's eyes that was barely visible from where Tracie stood. In her hands, she held a flattened brown paper bag. The puppy was yapping for all he was worth while snapping at the old lady's legs.

Tracie calmed herself slightly and tried to get the dog to do the same. But she kept her eye on the old woman. She was still baffled as to how she got in. She was sure she locked and bolted that back door. Extremely puzzled and confused she let it go at the sight of the little bent over, old lady. How much of threat could she be? She thought.

"Oh. Oh. I see. Uh, that's quite all right. I, uh, I'm just a little jumpy. I didn't expect to see anyone standing there and you really frightened me." Tracie bent to scoop up the little puppy from the floor. As she was struggling to hold on to the puppy, he was fighting equally as hard to get at the old lady. Never had Tracie seen him act this aggressive before. It was disturbing.

"Now you just stop that Kibble. It's only a lady who got lost. That's all. Now stop all that yapping." Her mind was still not settled about the back door.

"Look deary, I'm really sorry, don't let me impose on you any longer. I'll be getting on. But, uh, could you direct me to Clara Woodson's house? I could have sworn it was in this neighborhood but I guess it's not."

Try as she might to seem pleasant and apologetic, the dog wouldn't go for it. He wriggled out of Tracie's arms and ran in between the old lady's legs just as she was about to take a step. The old lady got entangled in her floor length skirt, tripped, and fell to the floor.

"Whoa!" she said as she hit the hard wood. Miraculously, she managed to save the pie as she fell. It never touched the floor.

"Oh my goodness. Now look what you've done, Kibble. You've knocked the poor lady down with your shananagans. Come here you bad little puppy." Again she scooped the dog up into her arms and this time she administered a light tap on the dog's hind quarters which didn't phase him in the least. He continued to bark and snap at the old woman.

"I'm terribly sorry ma'am. I don't know what's gotten into him." She proceded to help the old woman up from the floor where she had fallen. The dog continued to bark incessantly, make snapping motions with its mouth at the old woman. The old woman was obviously angry at the dog but tried to suppress her anger.

"Oh that couldn't be helped. I'm all right.", she said as she attempted to straighten the gray wig on her head. "But it seems my pie has been ruined." She turned her attention to the brown bag held high in her hand. Getting up with the help of Tracie, she managed to put the bag on the table and open it up so that the entire pie was exposed to Tracie's eyes.

Tracie was immediately drawn to the smell and took a step closer to look at it as well as to get a better smell. The old woman glared at Tracie as she awaited for Tracie's reaction.

"Oh my word. It is messed up. But just a little. It's not all that bad!" Tracie said.

She was unable to take her eyes off the pie. It was irresistible. The smell, tantalized her.

"Oh yes it is. I wouldn't think of giving such a mess to my dear friend. I'll just have to throw it away. But wait! It would be a shame to waste such a delicious, fresh baked, apple pie. Why don't you just have it. You have been such a sweet little girl to me, why don't you just keep it. I would be ever so grateful." The old woman looked at Tracie with eyes that were meant to entice. She was doing all she could to tempt little Tracie into accepting the pie.

"Oh I wouldn't think of it...but... my goodness it just...it smells so good." Tracie was mesmerized by the sight and aroma of the delicious looking pie.

"Oh don't be so stupid," the old lady blurted out. "I mean, how could *I* be so stupid. I should have known better than to think you'd take something that was meant for an-other. Please forgive me, but, listen, why not just take a piece then..."

Tracie could no longer resist. She quickly accepted before the old lady could finish her invitation. Using her fingers, she scooped up a large piece of the pie that had been smashed and gobbled it up as though she were starving.

My! Ummm, Oh my! Ummmm. Ummmm. That is good. I mean that is really good."

The old lady smiled a wicked smile. Pleased to see her plan work out so well. She had a glimmer in her eye that belied the purest of delights.

"Boy. Oh boy, with some ice cream? Man! This pie would be gone in a second." Tracie remarked, clearly taken with the taste of the tainted pie.

"Hmmmm. Ice cream. Yasssss. Well, you may as well eat it all now, honey. 'Cause I sure don't want it. Hey, look, kid. You've been kind. I'll be moving along now. Enjoy!" And without further ado, the old lady disappeared as stealthily as she appeared. Tracie could hardly stop stuffing the pie in her mouth to say goodbye. The puppy continued to bark. Tracie continued to gorge herself on the pie until there was only a sliver left on the plate.

"Oh boy! I'm stuffed. I got to sit my greedy butt down. Whew! I'm really stuffed. Wow! I'm getting sleepy. Man, Kibble, I can hardly...keep my eyes op...." And she fell to the floor.

The old lady's work was as yet complete. She still had the bumbling killers to deal with. She managed to make it to the street where they live. She spotted the old green Volkswagen van without a problem.

"Ah!" she said aloud, "there's that bucket of bolts those stupid suckers ride around in. I'll just put these special friends of mine in the cab to greet them when they get in it in the morning. Lets see how tricky they are then. With that, she released five poisonous rattle snakes into the vehicle. And just as a shadow moves along the ground, she slithered away. Quietly laughing her wicked, evil laugh.

CHAPTER 10
FRIENDS SHOW THEY CARE

Two and a half weeks passed before the little people returned. They were in the best of spirits when their old, raggedy truck pulled up to the curb in front of their house. They had the music blaring, and they were all singing and jovial. Surprisingly, they were already cleaned up. And they all had a present or some sort of gift that they planned to give to their little house guests.

As they embarked, they began to bicker among themselves about who was to be the first to present her with the present. As they argued over who would go into the house first, Money managed to get their attention with a loud whistle.

"Hey. Hey hold up. Now just stop it! All of y'all are acting just like a bunch of kids. Look at you. What is y'all doing?" All the while, he was inching his way toward the door. Scoota picked up on his intentions and made a dash to beat him to the door, this caused all of them to run for the door.

The door was open and as they reached it the first one fell and the rest fell on top of him and there they were. Piled up on one another. They scrambled to get to their feet but the first one to reach the kitchen was Stutter. He stopped dead in his tracks, as did everyone behind him.

"L-l-l-l-l-look!", he said. He was in disbelief at what he saw before him.

All eyes focused on the crumpled body on the floor. They gathered around her. Money pushed his way through them and dropped down on his knees and attempted to revive her but to no avail. After several attempts, he felt her pulse and held his hand over her heart one last time. He looked up with a tear in his eye and told them that...she was dead.

They immediately suspected her evil stepsister and they began to talk about how they were going to avenge her untimely death. All of a sudden it became clear to Scoota the reality of the situation they were in.

"Hold on fellas! You know what? Dig this. We in trouble. I don't know if y'all noticed or not but, this could easily look like we did it. I mean, think about it. How are we supposed to prove that this supposedly *evil stepsister* did this? And secondly, how do we even know she even *exists*? You see what I'm sayin'?" Scoota was dumbstruck with this revelation.

"Yeah, Scoota, I see what you mean. Like if we come out sayin' that somebody we don't even know exists came in here and killed her, then, how we gonna prove it. Right?" Funky was proud of his contribution to the mystery, but Scoota and Money were unimpressed.

"Brilliant thinking bright boy!" Scoota remarked, sarcastically.

"But anyway, it's not gonna to look good for us if we tell anybody that we got a dead body in our house. And on top of it, a house that we don't own and ain't even supposed to be in.
And on top of *that*...the dead body of a *beautiful young girl*. Wow."

The still figure that lay in their midst, drove home the enormity of the problem they were faced with. Calmly, Money attempted to put it all in perspective.

"Yeah. Scoota. My man. You got a good point there. What you actually sayin' is that it ain't no way we could go to the police, or nobody else, for that matter, and report a murder in our house. We probably would be the major suspects."

Money was unable to continue due to the constant wailing coming from Honey.

"Oh my baby. My baby, who did this to you. Oh..."

On and on, on and on she continued to cry as she was finally led away from the body. Poota, being the one who was helping her, but as he did so....

"S'cuse me."

Everyone looked at him with much disgust and surprise, yet, no one said a word. They just headed quickly for the back door. Honey also had broken free of his grasp to escape the pungent smell of his gas.

"Aw come on Poota. How could you?", Money asked, "how could you do that at a time like this?"

They allowed plenty of time for the air to clear before they cautiously crept back in. Once inside and the air tested breathable again, Scoota noticed something.

"Hey! Wait a minute. Look! There ain't no blood. No blood nowhere." They began to look on her and around her. Not a speck of blood could be found. Now they were forced to ponder the alleged murder all over again.

"You right, Scoota." Money concurred, "So what happened? Maybe she wasn't killed! Maybe she just fell out and killed herself!"

Honey again bursts into tears and loud crying. Again someone lead her away from the body.

"Look," Money continued, "We all know that none of us in here did it. Right? 'Cause we was in Delaware." They agreed in unison. "Ok. So what we got to do is put her up for a while. I mean hide her body for a bit until we can come up with some clues. Then we can figure out some things and put some things together. I got it. Look. I know this dude whose father is a funeral director, see. And what I can do, see, is get wit' him tomorrow and see if he can put the body on ice or somethin' for a couple of days until we can find out somethin'. Huh?"

Money was pleased with his idea. He looked around for approval from the others that it was a good plan. They all nodded in agreement.

"That's a pretty good idea, Moneyman! But...what we gone do with her now?" Scoota asked.

"Well, for now, I suggest we just put her on the sofa, you know, like she sleepin'.

"And in the mornin' we can just pick her up and take her out." They agreed with Money's suggestion. That night, none of them were able to sleep. They sat up around her still body. Silently. Solemnly. With tear stained faces.

Morning came quickly and Money left early to arrive at the Freeman's Funeral Parlor. He rang the bell and patiently waited for someone to answer. Fortunately, it was Christophor who answered the door.

"Yo! Money? What's happpenin'? Dag man, what you doin' up so early in the mornin'?" He looked closely at Money's face.

"Uh oh! Somethin' *must* be wrong."

Money checked up and down the street making sure they weren't seen, then, he pushed Chris back inside.

"Hold on Chris. Let's talk inside."

Once inside he continued. "Now Chris, you got to believe this. It's all true..."

And he related the entire story to Chris. After he finished talking, Chris sank deep in his chair. He seemed to be in a state of shock.

"Whoa, man! Wow! This is really deep. I mean this is heavy. Now wait a minute. Where is this chick now?

"Right now she at our spot on the sofa...pretending to be sleep!", Money sheepishly replied. Chris was puzzled by Money's response but continued getting dressed.

"Let's go!" Chris said. And they left out, headed for the house in the park.

Upon their arrival, Chris took but one look at the angelic face of the young girl and recognized her immediately. He stopped, and stood cold still. He could only stare in disbelief.

"Whoa! I know this chick. I mean I seen her before. One day when I was up in the rich folks' neighborhood. Dag, man this is wild!", he said emphatically, "I can't believe this. Okay, wait a minute. Let's just back up a little bit. Okay. So, then what she told y'all must be true. See, I was at her house one time but she was crying and all and I didn't get a chance to say what I wanted to say to her. But I'll never forget that face. I been back up there a thousand times tryin' to get back with her. But every time, this mean old chick with a mole on her chin kept tellin' me that she didn't live there. I knew somethin' was wrong. Yeah man. I know exactly where she live. Or used to live, rather, I mean...Oh never mind, give me a hand gettin' her into the hearse. We'll take her to the parlor and I'll sneak her in somewhere 'til we can find out something to tell my pop. Come on.

They moved Tracie to Chris's father's funeral parlor where Chris located the only available coffin.

It seems the only coffin that wasn't being used was one that had been designed for a play they were helping out the church with. It was plastic but was meant to appear as clear glass. You could see right through it. They put her in it and covered it back up.

Two days elapsed and Chris could keep the secret no longer. He had to tell his father. Despite their sincere attempts to bring about a resolution to their problem, they came up empty handed.

When he finally revealed the body to his father, he was perplexed, to say the least. He pondered the situation. Rationalizing that she had no family and the body had been cold for several days, he reasoned that it was best to begin to prepare to bury her. They both reluctantly agreed and began the embalming process. Money and the others were sent to alert the proper authorities.

Chris prepared the embalming fluid and as he carried it to where Tracie's body lay, he tripped over a cord causing a drop of the liquid somehow to fling, drop, spill or whatever but it, somehow, landed on the lips of the still, young body. This drop of fluid proved to be the antidote for the *Zombie Powder* mixture that Tracie ingested. Who would ever have suspected? He watched in amazement as Tracie's body twitched. Then jerked.

Her eyelids fluttered, then, popped open. The next thing he knew, she was fully awake. Chris saw this but he didn't believe it. He stood there with the container held tightly in his hands. Then, as if on cue, he screamed and fainted. Falling straight to the floor beneath Tracie's cot.

Tracie recognized *him* immediately. She struggled to sit up and managed to look down upon *his* now-still body.

"Oh my goodness. What have I done?", she queried At the same time, she realized that she didn't even know where she was. Let alone what she was doing there or why he was stretched out on the floor. She slid her legs over the side of the cot and leaned over Chris who was just beginning to regain consciousness. He strained to focus on the face that was staring into his. She looked directly into his eyes.

"Oh good. You're okay. I didn't mean to frighten you. I..."

Chris heard her voice but it was as if she were talking in a tunnel or a can or something.

"I-I-I-I-I-I, we-we-we-we-we, they- they, I, we, thought you were, uh, *dead*?", he mumbled. Chris tried to speak but his words were all jumbled up. He could not believe what had just taken place.

"Dead?" Tracie exclaimed in horror. She was just as surprised as Chris. "What are you talking about? Why would anyone think I was dead? I only went to sleep for a little while, and now I wake up here in this strange place. What am I doing here anyway? And who are you?"

As she was fully alert now, these questions seemed perfectly normal to her. She was even becomming indignant toward Chris. Chris, all the while, was still trying to gather his senses as well as to get over his astonishment at Tracie's overpowering beauty.

"Waaaait a minute! Hold up. Somethin's fishy here. You say you only been *"sleep"* for a little while? Tell me, can you remember what you were doing before you went to...uh...*"sleep"*?" He seemed to be trying to put together a theory that would put things in perspective for him and make things much clearer to understand.

"Well." Tracie said hesitantly. "Lets see. I remember eating some pie...some apple pie. And that's the last thing I remember." She tried hard to recall the events that preceded her *nap*.

"Wait a minute! You say you remember that you ate some pie or something? Where did you get this pie from?" As Chris was being helped to his feet, he was more interested in getting to the bottom of this mystery.

"I remember now. This sweet old lady came to the house by accident and gave it to me!"

"Oh yeah. What did this *"sweet old lady"* look like? Can you describe her?" Chris instinctively felt he was on to something. He felt it in his heart.

"Uh. No. Not really. Except she was old and bent over. Oh! She did have a mole. Right here on her chin." Tracie pointed to the spot on *her* chin where she remembered the mole to be on the old lady's chin. Chris began to put it together now.

"A mole? Did you say a mole on her chin? There was a nasty woman at the house where you used to live that had a big-ole', ugly mole on her chin too! I remember, 'cause I hate moles, especially big ones on people's chins with hair coming all out of it and stuff. Her's was so big there was no way you could miss it."

"Evellia!" Tracie remembered, "Evellia! My step-sister. That's right. She *does* have a mole on her chin. But how did you know that?" She was curious as to how Chris would have known about her stepsister. Chris looked up at her with a boyish look on his face.

"I saw you one time I was lost up there in your neighborhood and you were on the front stoop. You were crying and you looked so sad, yet, you looked so beautiful. I never forgot you or where you lived. So I went back up there lookin' for you. Actually, I went back up there a lot of times hopin' to see you again. But each time I only got to see the mean old nasty face of that lady. Evellia, or whatever her name is.

I seen her enough to know what she looks like. But listen, I know about your problem. Your little friends are the ones that told me all about you and what was happening with you. I'm beginning to suspect that it had to be her. I think she may have disguised herself as an old woman and she must have poisoned the pie with something. Somehow, she must have found out where you were staying and got in there and gave you that poisoned pie." Chris was almost sure his theory was fairly accurate.

"Darn. I have this awful taste in my mouth." She wiped her mouth and distorted her face as if she just ate a lemon. Chris looked at her strangely then asked her.

"Come here. Closer! Let me smell your lips." He was tempted to kiss her lips as she got them nearer to his face. But he restrained himself. "Hmmmm. That smell. It's the liquid fluid we use to embalm people! I must have spilled some of it on you and somehow it got into your mouth and into your system thereby reversing the effects of whatever it was that she put in that pie. Come on. We got some work to do."

He pulled Tracie by the hand, almost dragging her out of the laboratory and off to the house in the park.

The little guys were sad, and sullen. Stutter answered the door and upon seeing Tracie, he was more speechless than he already had been.

"H-h-h-h-h-h-h-h-hey! Y-y-y-y-y-y-you're s'posed to be d-d-d-d-d-d-d-dead!!!" He shivered as he stood in the door, unable to move. He stood there pointing his finger at Tracie as Chris brushed by him dragging Tracie with him. The others heard him and came to the vestibule door. They too, gawked at her with open mouths and wide eyes. Then Poota broke the silence.

"S'cuse me" he quietly warned"

Everybody, including Tracie broke for the outside. But Chris didn't. Only because he didn't know about Poota's deadly gas attacks. Once outside, they began to hoop and holler and rejoice over Tracie's revival. Suddenly, Tracie remembered Chris.

"Hey wait a minute. Where's Chris?", she asked. Just at that moment they looked toward the door and poor Chris was standing there holding his head.

"Man. Why didn't somebody tell me? Wow! Once it hit me, I bolted for the door and ran smack into the wall. Boy, that was horrible. Does he do that all the time?"

Poota felt obliged to answer. "Naw. Only when I can't hold it in."

Everybody laughed and began filing back into the house.

"Well look fellas, we got us a problem..."

Chris took the time to relate his theory to them about Evellia and the pie. Everyone appeared to be pondering the theory. Finally, they agreed that it made sense to them.

CHAPTER 11
TRACIE'S VICTORY

While Chris and the boys were busy devising a plan, Evellia was busy talking to a Life Insurance agent.

"Now, you're sure I won't have any problems taking out such a large policy on my poor little sister, right?

"Of course not, Ms. Evans, as a matter of fact, I would have *recommended* that you do so if you hadn't. You see..." Evellia interrupted him mid-sentence.

"Good. Okay. You got my money now alls y'all got to do is pay up if something happens to her. 'Cause I heard that insurance companies love to get people's money, but they hate to pay people when the time comes. Okay. Thank you so much, Mr., Uh, what's your name again?" She began gathering the agent's coat and hat as she asked him his name while she pushed him toward the door.

"Henderson, Geo..."

Again, she rudely, interrupted him.

"Yeah, right, Mr. Henderson. Whatever! Okay. I'll be talking to you." She managed to get him out of the door as she handed him his coat and hat. Then she promptly closed the door in his face. That done, she turned to her mirrors and started thinking aloud, as she usually does.

"Excellent! Now alls I got to do is get to that Freeman's Funeral Home in a day or so and claim that stinking little misfit's body. It's a good thing I kept tabs on those little suckers or I would never have known that. But, you can't pull the wool over these beautiful eyes. I'll have her in the ground so fast it's going to make her head spin. Then it's off to the Baltimore Law Offices to get my rightful inheritance money. Oooooooweeee! I'm gonna be so filthy rich that I won't ever have to speak to nobody if I don't want to. Well, except maybe for those filthy rich men who are going to be all over this beautiful hunk of woman I see standing before me."

Soon, she became totally absorbed in one of her mirror adventures. Who knows how long she had been admiring herself when, the doorbell rang.

"Who the heck could that be?" she wondered, "I ain't expecting nobody here."

Reluctantly, she tore herself away from her image and sauntered over to the door. She nonchalantly looked out of the peephole. Straining to see, she was unable to make out the figure standing on the other side.

"Who the heck is that? I don't want any. Go away."

She heard a faint voice through the door, so she curiously looked again.

"Who is that? I can't see you?" This time she recognized the voice but didn't believe it.

"It's me Evellia. Open the door. It's me...Tracie."

Upon hearing the name, she backed away from the door staring at it as though she could see right through it.

"Who? Tracie? Bull!! You ain't no Tracie."

Unsure whether it was or not, she could not restrain her curiosity. She stepped boldly to the door and snatched it open. What she saw made her cringe with fear at first. It was truly Tracie, but she was made up to appear ghostly. She had powder white skin, tattered clothing and a blank stare in her blackened eyes. Her arms were outstretched to Evellia.

"Yes, Evellia, it's me. I have come to stay with you...forever."

Evellia backed away from the door.

"Noooooo!!" she screamed, "This can't be true. You can't be alive. I put enough Zombie Powder in that pie to put you to sleep forever."

"It's true Evellia, I'm dead now and I have come back to stay with you forever."

Tracie persisted and took a step toward her. Evellia stepped back but she assumed her mean old disposition. She turned and ran to the kitchen to grab the first thing she could put her grubby little hands on. Then, she insanely charged the door with a meat cleaver held high in her hand as though she were going to chop up some meat.

"Noooooo. You little demon. Even in death you cause me problems. I'll get rid of you for good this time. I'll chop you up into so many little pieces that they won't ever be able to find you, you little, wretch."

She continued to advance towards Tracie, who at this point, was about to run. But just at that moment, Chris, the police, and the little people rushed past her and re-strained Evellia.

"No you won't Evellia. You've killed your *own* self this time. Arrest her officers!", Chris told the police, "you heard her confession."

Chris held Tracie tight in his arms and comforted her while the police carted the evil Evellia off to an awaiting squad car.

"Well, it looks like she's off to a new home and it looks like you got your old home back." He smiled lovingly at Tracie while looking around the house. Then he said, "But, you know? It don't look nothing like I would have imagined it looked in here!"

"I know," said Tracie, "this is Evellia's idea of decorating. I have a lot of work to do to get it back to the way I remember it. The way it was before."

"No." Scoota chimed in, "*We*, have a lot of work to do. You know you can count on us to help you whip this place back into shape. We'll have this crib lookin' sharp in no time."

As he and the others were talking about how happy they were that everything turned out for the good and their little family could return to normal, they heard Poota's faint little voice in the background.

"S'cuse me!" Of course everybody dashed for the door. Including Chris this time.

"Hey wait, y'all. I was only going to say that I was going to help too!"

Everybody just stopped where they were and laughed, relieved to know that his little "S'cuse me" didn't mean what it usually meant.

FINAL CHAPTER
TRACIE'S TRUE INHERITANCE

The Freeman's home was alive with laughter. The entire family was gathered together in the one room. Everyone truly enjoyed Scoota's story. They were having a great laugh at the way he ended it Everyone except little Brittany. She had fallen asleep at some point during the story. Suddenly, she woke up.

"Hey!" She exclaimed, "What happened. I was dreaming that I was seeing the whole story but I didn't even realize that I had fallen to sleep. Wow."

Scoota, and the others just looked at her with looks of disgust on their faces.

"Yeah. Okay. You'll know the next time I tell *you* a story.", said Scoota.

"Yeah," said Tracie, "and you got some nerve going to sleep like that. But you know what? After listening to Uncle Scoota talking about that great adventure in my life, I just realized something as I sat here looking around at this beautiful family, I realized that even though I got a lot of money through my inheritance, I really think that my real true inheritance is this family. If it wasn't for Uncle Scoota and his friends helping me when I needed help, and they were my family for a little while too, I would never have met your father. So, never forget, family and friends are truly a great inheritance.

"Okay kids, that's it, for real. Look at the time. It's ten o'clock. All people under four feet tall, upstairs...not you Scoota." She joked about Scoota's height because he was still short. He looked up at her and playfully tapped her arm. Chris laughed. And Tracie and the children started up the steps to be tucked in for bed.

"Hold it. I got a question!", said Marcus. "What ever happened to Aunt Evellia? Where she at now? And is she still in our family?"

Chris looked at Scoota and then to Tracie. Still with a puzzled look on his face he asked, "Do you know what? I believe she was sent to a Mental Health Rehabilitation facility for bad people and she had to stay there for 22 years. "And, after he gave it some more thought, "guess what else? That means she's due to come out...this year! They all looked at one another very strangely.

That very next day, it was a rainy, cloudy morning, and it was in another part of town, it was where the Metropolitan Mental Health Rehabilitation Facility was located, an old, fat, gray haired lady with a mole on her chin was being released and helped into a cab.

THE END

\